The Chameleon That Saved Noah's Ark

The Chameleon
That Saved
Noah's Ark

Yael Molchadsky

illustrated by
Orit Bergman

translated from Hebrew by
Annette Appel

Nancy Paulsen Books

In Noah's ark, there's such a commotion!
Donkeys bray, frogs croak, and lions roar.
Outside, the flood is raging.
Great drops of rain drum down on the roof.

Noah doesn't speak the language of the animals, but he listens and he knows: They are hungry. It is mealtime.

Noah climbs the ladder deep down into the pantry. His wife, Na'ama, and his sons are waiting for him. Together, they will prepare a meal for each and every animal.

A treat of meat for wild beasts,
grass and greens for the grazers,
and piles of seeds for the birds.

Na'ama wakes up at dawn to
make breakfast for the rooster,

and when darkness falls,
Noah feeds the creatures
of the night.

Only the two chameleons stare at them, their
eyes open wide, as if asking, "Where is our food?"
"Where, indeed?" wonder Noah and Na'ama.

They've tried to feed them everything—
seeds and roots, nuts and fruits—but they
refuse every dish.

"Look at the chameleon lying on the straw,"
Shem calls. "She's golden! And the one crawling
on the wood floor is brown. If they change colors,
maybe their tastes change, too?"

"Look at their humpy backs," says Ham.
"Maybe they store food inside, just like the camels?"

"And their neck is like a sack," adds Japheth.
"Maybe they save food in there, like the pelicans?"

"Maybe yes and maybe no," sighs Na'ama. "But meanwhile, they are getting thinner and thinner!"

"I will take one with me," Noah tells his sons, "and you will look after the other one. Let's watch them day and night until we find out what they like to eat!"

Noah holds out his hand and the chameleon slowly climbs up his arm and sits on his shoulder.

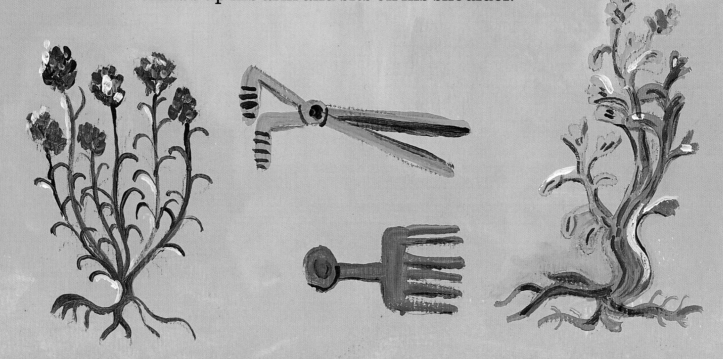

Whenever Noah eats something, he breaks off a crumb and offers it to the chameleon.

But she only sniffs at it and never opens her mouth.

"Well, to each his own," Noah says. "But I hope we will soon find out what you like to eat."

As the days go by, the chameleons get thinner and weaker. Noah can barely feel the one perched on his shoulder, and he watches her with a worried look on his face.

But an even greater worry awaits him down below in the ark's hold.

"Noah! Noah!" Na'ama calls as she quickly climbs up the ladder from the pantry. "I found worms in the fruit bins!"

She holds out half a pomegranate, and two little worms wiggle in between the seeds.

"What are we going to do?" Na'ama cries. "If we don't get rid of the worms, they will ruin all of the fruits and vegetables. Then what will we eat?"

Noah doesn't respond, but the chameleon has the answer. She opens her mouth, and out pops a long, sticky tongue. With a flick and a flash, she swallows both worms.

Noah and Na'ama look at each other in amazement. Big smiles spread across their faces.

"You saved us!" they exclaim.

The entire family hurries down the ladder into the ark's hold.

The boys place the two chameleons in the pantry bins and watch in awe as their fast tongues hungrily pick the worms off the fruits and vegetables.

"Oh, the wonders of nature!" Na'ama says.

"And we're keeping this wonder safe from the flood," Noah adds, "right here in the ark."

Then Noah picks up two worms and puts them in a bowl full of pomegranate seeds. "Even worms are little wonders," he whispers, "and we'll make sure to take care of you, too. Because soon, the sun will shine once again on the earth . . .

. . . and everything and everyone has a place under the sun."

In memory of Hadar Goldin,
who loved reading.

Nancy Paulsen Books
an imprint of Penguin Random House LLC
375 Hudson Street
New York, NY 10014

Manufactured in China by RR Donnelley Asia Printing Solutions Ltd.
ISBN 978-1-101-99676-8
10 9 8 7 6 5 4 3 2 1

Design by Annie Ericsson.
Text set in Parry Std.
The artwork was done in acrylic paint.